ALSO IN THE SERIES

Max Finder
MYSTERY
Collected Casebook

Volume 6

Distributed in Canada by University of Toronto Press
5201 Dufferin Street, Toronto, Ontario M3H 5T8

Distributed in the United States by Publishers Group West
1700 Fourth Street, Berkeley, California 94710

Library and Archives Canada Cataloguing in Publication

O'Donnell, Liam, 1970-
    Max Finder mystery : collected casebook / Liam O'Donnell, Michael Cho.

Vol. 6 by Craig Battle and Ramón Pérez.
Vol. 5-6 issued also in electronic format.
ISBN 978-1-926973-22-7 (bound : v. 6).--ISBN 978-1-926973-21-0 (pbk. : v. 6)

    1. Detective and mystery comic books, strips, etc. 2. Mystery games.
I. Cho, Michael II. Battle, Craig, 1980- III. Pérez, Ramón IV. Title.

PN6733.O36M38 2006   j741.5'971   C2006-903300-5

Library of Congress Control Number: 2009935531

Series Design: John Lightfoot/Lightfoot Art & Design Inc.
Design and Art Direction: Barb Kelly

 Canadian Patrimoine
Heritage canadien

 Canada

 Ontario
Ontario Media Development
Corporation

Canada Council Conseil des Arts
for the Arts du Canada

ONTARIO ARTS COUNCIL
CONSEIL DES ARTS DE L'ONTARIO

Société de développement
de l'industrie des médias
de l'Ontario

We acknowledge the financial support of the Canada Council for the Arts, the Ontario Arts Council,
the Government of Canada through the Canada Book Fund (CBF) and the Government of Ontario
through the Ontario Media Development Corporation's Book Initiative for our publishing activities.

Manufactured by WKT Co. Ltd.
Manufactured in Shenzhen, Guangdong, China, in December 2011
Job #11CB2869

A   B   C   D   E   F

Owl kids Publisher of Chirp, chickaDEE and OWL
www.owlkids.com

Max Finder

MYSTERY

Collected Casebook

Volume 6

Craig Battle and Ramón Pérez

Created by Liam O'Donnell

Owl kids

Contents

Top Secret Character Lineup 11

Comics

The Case of the Green Crime Scene 15

The Case of the Ghastly Ghost Walk 21

The Case of the Gaming Gaffe 27

The Case of the Suspicious Set 39

The Case of the Garage Sabotage 45

The Case of the Comic-Con Con 51

The Case of the Toilet Paper Prank 57

The Case of the Copycat Crime 69

The Case of the
  Birthday Party Treachery 75

The Case of the Daydreaming Detective ... 81

Stories

The Case of the Swimming Pool Stakeout.. 33

The Case of the Odd Job Shadow............. 63

Extra Stuff

Host Your Own Mystery Party.................. 89

Meet the Creators 94

Easy Ways to Use

Max Finder in the Classroom................ 95

Collected
Casebook
Volume 6

HEY, MYSTERY BUFFS!

Did you know that the book in your hands features a whopping ten comics and two short stories? Max Finder here, fact collector and junior-high detective. In our hometown of Whispering Meadows, my best friend, Alison, and I are the go-to investigators of mysteries big and small. This casebook collects some of our best moments yet.

From the **Green Crime Scene** all the way to the **Daydreaming Detective**, each mystery is crammed with enough clues, suspects, and red herrings to keep you guessing until the end. We've done all the legwork, but solving the mystery is up to you! Read the mysteries, watch for the clues, and try to crack the case. Solutions are at the end of each comic. But remember: real detectives never peek.

So fire up your mystery radar and get solving!

Max

P.S. Check out the lineup on page 11 to get the inside scoop on the characters of Whispering Meadows, and go to page 89 to learn how to host your own mystery party!

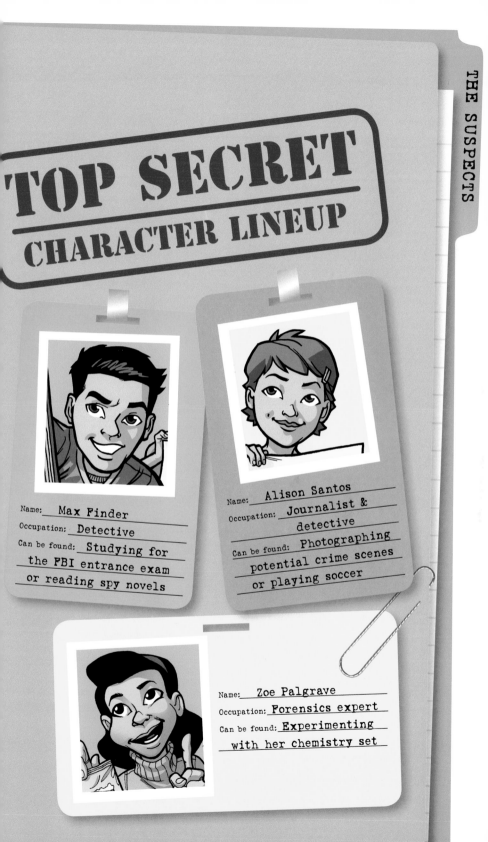

TOP SECRET
CHARACTER LINEUP

Name: __Max Finder__
Occupation: __Detective__
Can be found: __Studying for__
__the FBI entrance exam__
__or reading spy novels__

Name: __Alison Santos__
Occupation: __Journalist &__
__detective__
Can be found: __Photographing__
__potential crime scenes__
__or playing soccer__

Name: __Zoe Palgrave__
Occupation: __Forensics expert__
Can be found: __Experimenting__
__with her chemistry set__

Name: Ben "Basher" McGintley
Occupation: Usual suspect
Can be found: Bullying around town

Name: Ana Guzman
Occupation: New girl in town
Can be found: At her parents' game store

Name: Jake Granger
Occupation: Magician
Can be found: Sneaking up behind Max and Alison

Name: Leslie Chang
Occupation: Gossip
Can be found: Keeping everyone else in line

Name: Dorothy Pafko

Occupation: Co-captain of the Green Thumb Club

Can be found: In the science lab

Name: Stuart DeSilva

Occupation: Gamer

Can be found: In the computer lab

Name: Myron Matthews

Occupation: Aspiring detective

Can be found: Six steps behind Max

Name: Jessica Peeves

Occupation: Local royalty, a.k.a. the mayor's daughter

Can be found: Planning parties

13

Name: Sasha Price
Occupation: Self-proclaimed
local celebrity
Can be found: By the pool

Name: Alex Rodriguez
Occupation: Perfectionist
Can be found: Playing trivia
(and winning)

Name: Tony DeMatteo
Occupation: Hockey and
football star
Can be found: Hanging out
with his older brother

Name: Crystal Diallo
Occupation: Dog walker
Can be found: Reading or
drawing manga

Max Finder, junior-high detective, here. It was a Wednesday morning in the new school year. Green Thumb Club heads Dorothy Pafko and Jeff Coleman had entered a national video contest to prove we were the greenest school around, and my best friend, Alison, and I were helping out.

WITH ALISON'S PHOTOGRAPHY SKILLS AND THE CAMERA EQUIPMENT FROM YOUR MOM'S TV STATION, MAX, THERE'S NO WAY WE CAN LOSE!

MAX, I JUST WANT TO BEAT TWINDALE! THOSE LOUDMOUTHS HAVE BEEN TALKING ABOUT HOW THEY'RE GOING TO TRASH US IN THIS CONTEST.

DON'T WORRY, JEFF. THEY JUST WANT TO WIN THE GRAND PRIZE. THAT VIDEO-EDITING SUITE WOULD BE PRETTY AWESOME.

We had already filmed segments for our school's cafeteria compost program and the litterless lunch campaign, and now we were outside to check out the school's community garden.

THREE, TWO, ONE... ACTION!

YOU WANT A SCHOOL THAT'S REALLY "GREEN"? HOW ABOUT A SCHOOL THAT GROWS ITS OWN GREENS? COME ON AND...

SHOO!

ANNOYING BIRDS!

CUT!

First I was concerned about the ruined shot, but then I noticed the garden was in much worse shape.

UH-OH...

YOU SAID IT, JEFF. LOOKS LIKE SOMEONE GROUND UP THE GARDEN.

The school field acts as an unofficial dog park during the evening. We returned that night to talk to some dog walkers and quickly saw one of our oldest enemies.

LUKAS HAJDUK, WHAT BRINGS YOU HERE? DON'T YOU GO TO TWINDALE?

YEAH, BUT I LIVE AROUND THE CORNER. I WALK MY DOG HERE EVERY NIGHT.

YOU WOULDN'T HAPPEN TO HAVE SEEN ANYONE OVER IN THE GARDEN LAST NIGHT, WOULD YOU?

YEAH, RIGHT. LIKE I'M KEEPING TABS ON YOUR STUPID GARDEN...

LOOK OUT! RUNAWAY HUSKY!

What is this, a Max Finder Nemes[es] Convention? Jake Granger loves two things: 1) magic tr[icks] and 2) competing [with] me to solve myste[ries]. Right now, though, [he] looked like he just wanted to catch h[is]

WHOA!

MAX! HEEL!

HUH?

whine

NOT YOU, FINDER. MY DOG'S NAME IS ALSO MAX.

Jake told us he's terrible with dogs, so his parents make him do dog-walking duty only once a week. Luckily, Crystal Diallo was around to save the day. She has a dog-walking business and is the best handler in town.

I WISH I COULD HELP YOU GUYS, BUT I WASN'T HERE LAST NIGHT. I HAD TO WALK MRS. BRIGGS'S BULLDOG, PEACHES, AROUND THE BLOCK.

RUFF RUFF RUFF RUFF

After I dusted myself off, we headed back over the garden, where Jeff was hard at work.

YOU GUYS SHOULD TALK TO JAKE. HE PLAYS CAPTURE THE FLAG HERE ON TUESDAY NIGHTS. WE ASKED HIM TO STOP PLANTING FLAGS IN THE GARDEN, BUT HE DIDN'T LIKE THAT VERY MUCH!

YOU COM[E] NEXT WEEK, YOU WERE MVP LA[ST] GAME!

SOLUTION:

THE CASE OF THE...
GREEN CRIME SCENE

Who trashed the garden?

Peaches. Crystal tied Peaches up by the field so she could play Capture the Flag, but Peaches chewed through the leash and got into the garden. Crystal felt so bad about it she tried to cover it up.

Clues

- Crystal said she wasn't at the field the night before, but Jake said she was the MVP of the last game of Capture the Flag. She was lying to Max to make herself look innocent.

- The chewed-through leash was the same type that Crystal was using to walk the three dogs. In fact, Max noticed that there was a small price tag still on one of them. Crystal needed to replace the one Peaches ruined the night before.

- Alison noticed that Peaches likes to chase birds. She remembered that earlier in the day, Jeff had to shoo birds out of the garden, which explained why Peaches would go there. Once the birds flew away, Peaches chewed up the garden.

- According to Zoe, both Peaches (a bulldog) and Jake's dog, Max (a Siberian husky), could

have made the bite marks on the stake. However, because Jake wa his dog only once a week, he wo not have had Max at the field th night the garden was trashed.

- Lukas Hajduk's dog, a Great Da is much too large and strong to leave the bite marks of a mid-si dog.

- Jeff may have been meddling wi the crime scene, but he didn't s any evidence. Crystal was one o the kids at the crime scene in th morning, and she had the stake her back pocket as she walked a

Conclusion

Max presented his evidence and Crystal came clean—she felt terri about Peaches tearing up the gar on her watch. She enlisted everyo from Capture the Flag to help the Green Thumb Club prepare the garden for the video, and Centra Meadows went on to win the cont

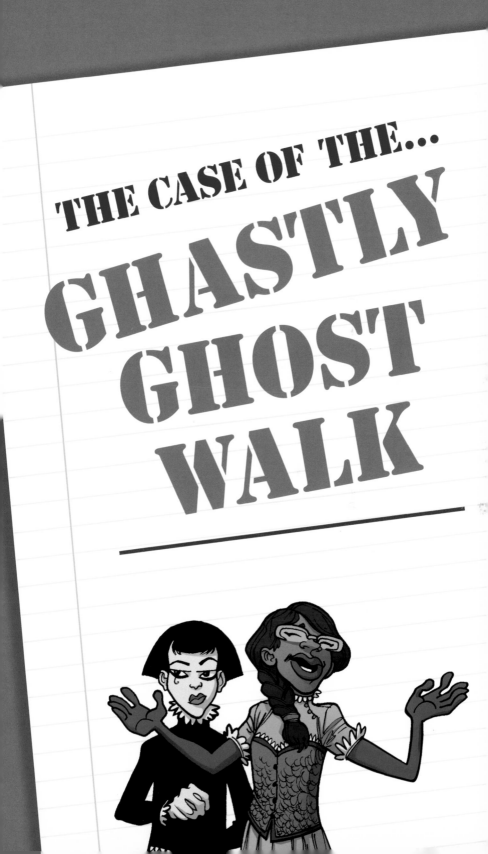

THE CASE OF THE...

GHASTLY GHOST WALK

THE CASE OF THE...
GHASTLY GHOST WALK

Max Finder, junior-high detective, here. When our friend Jay Rogers came to Alison and me saying she'd seen something "terrifyingly awful" in a dumpster, I was less than excited about the case.

ARE YOU SURE YOU DIDN'T SEE SOMETHING "TERRIFYINGLY AWFUL" AT THE COMIC SHOP OR THE VIDEO GAME STORE?

VERY FUNNY, MAX! NOW COME OVER HERE AND HELP US LIFT THIS.

SLAM AAHHHHH

WELL, JAY, LOOKS LIKE WE GOT YOUR GHOST. CASE CLOSED.

I NEVER THOUGHT THE GHOST WAS REAL, MAX. SOMEONE USED THIS TO RUIN THE FIRST NIGHT OF THE GHOST WALK THAT ALISON'S BROTHER IS ORGANIZING.

So there was a mystery after all. Alison's brother, Marcus, and his friends Annette and Michaela just started a new ghost walk around our town. Last ni was the first walk, but apparently it didn't go we

MARCUS HASN'T TOLD ME MUCH, BUT THE GHOST WALK IS SUPPOSED TO BE MORE HISTORICAL AND LESS HAUNTED HOUSE.

IF THE WALK ISN MEANT TO SCAR THEN THIS IS N RANDOM PRANK. I SABOTAGE. TELL WHAT HAPPENED L NIGHT, JAY.

We had no idea why someone involved in the ghost walk would want to sabotage it, but we were determined to find out—fast. Alison couldn't get Marcus on the phone, so we tracked Michaela down at the library.

DO YOU KNOW WHO MIGHT HAVE BEEN BEHIND LAST NIGHT'S SABOTAGE?

I CAN THINK OF TWO PEOPLE. THE FIRST IS ANNETTE. SHE WANTED TO DO A SCARY GHOST WALK FROM THE BEGINNING, BUT MARCUS AND I OUTVOTED HER. SHE COULD STILL BE MAD.

PERIODICALS

THE SECON... BRIAN. HE ... THE HAUN... HOUSE IN T... AND COULD E... FROM THE G... WALK GOING...

I BET YOU CAN FIND BOTH OF THEM AT THE INTERNET CAFÉ. BRIAN WORKS THERE AND ANNETTE'S THERE 24/7 VIDEO CHATTING WITH HER BOYFRIEND.

THANKS, MICHAELA. DO YOU HAVE ANY IDEA WHERE WE CAN FIND MARCUS?

HE WAS ACTUALLY RIGHT HERE A SECOND AGO. HE SORT OF TOOK OFF WHEN HE SAW YOU GUYS COMING.

Alison was steamed that Marcus was ducking us, you know what they say: "The case must go on!" ... found Brian at the café and asked him if he knew anything about last night's "ghost."

ONLY 2 DAYS LEFT UNTIL THE
HAUNTED HOUS...
BE THERE OR BE S...
FOR MORE INFO...
CALL CASPER
@ 555-47...

INTERNI
CAFÉ

BRIAN

SORRY, GUY... A PILLOWCAS... GHOST? ANY K... TOWN COULD ... THAT TOGETH...

WHILE WE'RE HERE, DO YOU MIND TELLING US WHAT YOU WERE DOING LAST NIGHT?

I WAS SCARING KIDS DOWN AT THE HAUNTED HOUSE. YOU GUYS SHOULD CHECK IT OUT.

THE GHOST WALK IS A JOKE!

THAT SOUNDS LIKE ANNETTE...

MICHAELA'S SO BOSSY, AND MARCUS DOESN'T EVEN LOOK LIKE HE WANTS TO BE THERE! MAYBE I'LL JUST PULL THE BIGGEST PRANK OF ALL AND MAKE MYSELF DISAPPEAR.

SHHHH!

SOLUTION:

THE CASE OF THE...
GHASTLY GHOST WALK

Who's messing with the ghost walk?

Brian Casperov. He sabotaged the ghost walk to eliminate competition for his haunted house, which was going to start in two days.

Clues

- Brian told Max that he was scaring kids at the haunted house on the night of the first ghost walk. However, a sign in the internet café said the haunted house hadn't started yet. He was lying.

- Basher said he was hired by someone named Casper. Max noticed that Brian's name tag said his last name was Casperov, and the sign announcing the haunted house said to call "Casper" for more info. Casper is Brian's nickname.

- Michaela said Annette video chats at the internet café all the time, and while Max and Alison were there, she was revealing details about the ghost walk. That explains how Brian would've learned the ghost walk route in order to plan his prank.

- There were a lot of Tenretni Café coffee cups in the dumpster when Max, Jay, and Alison found the pillowcase ghost. That's because the alley is next to the café. That

means Brian would have had acc to the roof to rig up a pulley syst

- Marcus was ducking Max and Ali because he had something to hid but it wasn't sabotaging the ghos walk. As Michaela told the crowd he had a bad case of stage fright and was embarrassed about it.

- Annette may have wanted a more scare-oriented ghost walk, but she didn't commit the crime. Accordin to Jay's testimony, she was talking t the crowd at the time of the prank wouldn't have been able to pull the rope to lift the lid of the dumpster.

Conclusion

When Max and Alison presented t evidence, Brian emerged from the shadows and confessed. He apolog for trying to sabotage the ghost wa and even offered to split the profit of the haunted house to make up f it. Annette, Michaela, and Marcus finished the ghost walk that night, and everyone walked away impress not to mention a little freaked out!

THE CASE OF THE...

GAMING GAFFE

THE CASE OF THE...
GAMING GAFFE

Max Finder, junior-high detective, here. Alison, Zoe, and I were at the rec center on Sunday to see kids compete at *Slo-Mo Kart*, the racing game. After a few minutes, we realized one thing: video game racing can be just as intense as real racing.

BETTER STICK TO YOUR VITAMINS, HOLLY. ALL YOU'RE EATING RIGHT NOW IS MY DUST!

DON'T COUNT YOUR MONEY YET, "GILLIONAIRE."

THAT'S ALL, FOLKS. THE WINNER IS HOLLY "VITAMIN H" STINSON!

BUMP

NO FAIR, HOLLY! THAT WAS A CHEAP SHOT! I'M OUTTA HERE!

HEY!

AND THIS CONCLUDES THE FIRST ROUND. THE HIGHEST SCORE SO FAR BELONGS TO...VITAMIN H! WE'LL TAKE A SHORT BREAK NOW AND BE BACK IN 30 MINUTES WITH ROUND TWO.

SEE, HOLLY! I TOLD YOU YOU'D WIN!

SEEMS LIKE HOLLY HAS A FAN. ETHAN WEBSTER HAS BEEN DITCHING HIS REC CENTER DUTIES ALL DAY TO CHEER HER ON!

A few minutes after the break started, word spread that Whispering Meadows' best pretzel truck was outside, and we all rushed out to get in line.

SAMIR SURE SEEMED MAD ABOUT LOSING TO HOLLY.

THAT'S BECAUSE HE WAS THE TOP-RANKED PLAYER ENTERING THE TOURNAMENT. HOLLY SURPRISED EVERYONE.

MAX! ALISON! WE NEED SOME DETECTIVES INSIDE, PRONTO.

little
we found
[St]uart had
to enter
[tou]rnament
[did]n't get his
[f]orm in on
[A]fter that,
[deci]ded to
[off]er to help
[Coa]ch Sweeny.

IT MUST HAVE MADE YOU PRETTY MAD THAT THE TOURNAMENT WOULDN'T MAKE AN EXCEPTION FOR YOU, HUH, STUART?

OF COURSE IT DID! I MEAN...UH, SORT OF. BUT I GOT OVER IT.

[...] WERE THE FIRST TO [...] THE GAME SYSTEMS [...EN] TAMPERED WITH. [...]ELSE WAS IN HERE WITH YOU?

SAMIR WAS IN THE STANDS EATING A CHOCOLATE BAR, AND COACH SWEENY WAS GLUED TO A MONITOR AT THE ORGANIZER'S TABLE. I'M SURPRISED HE DIDN'T SEE ANYTHING.

A few minutes later, our hour was almost up and Coach Sweeny was ready to throw in the towel.

YOU DID YOUR BEST, GUYS, BUT I THINK THIS IS ONE CASE THAT'S GOING TO REMAIN UNSOLVED. THOSE GAMES AND HARD DRIVES COULD BE ANYWHERE BY NOW.

WHOA! HOLD UP, COACH!

Bent Weathers

WHAT GIVES, ALISON?

ONE PERSON'S TRASH IS ANOTHER PERSON'S CASE-SOLVING CLUE, MAX. I KNOW WHO'S TAMPERING WITH THIS TOURNAMENT.

Do you know who stole the games and hard drives? All the clues are here. Turn the page for the solution.

THE CASE OF THE...
GAMING GAFFE

Who tampered with the tournament?

Samir Gill. He was angry because he got knocked out of the tournament, so he stole all the games and hard drives to shut it down. He also framed Ethan for the crime.

Clues

• "Bent Weathers" may be an anagram for "Ethan Webster," but when Alison saw the name on the disc, she recognized the handwriting as Samir's. It was an exact match to the writing from the name card Samir was wearing on his back.

• Ethan and Holly were outside in line at the pretzel stand while the crime went down, but Samir wasn't. He used the pretzel distraction to steal the games and hard drives.

• Stuart said Samir had been eating a chocolate bar in the stands shortly after the games and hard drives were stolen. That explains the brown fingerprint Alison saw on the disc—it was chocolate from Samir's hands.

• Coach Sweeny was inside at the time of the crime, as Stuart said, but he was watching a football game on his computer. That's why he didn't notice anything. It's also why he tried to get out of organizing the tournament.

Conclusion

When Alison presented her evidence, Samir confessed. He apologized for being a sore loser and returned the games and hard drives to Coach Sweeny. He had hidden them behind the large curtain at the front of the room, and had dropped his chocolate bar wrapper in front of the curtain when he did. The gaming tournament continued, and Vitamin H wound up winning after all...fair and square!

The Case of the
Swimming Pool Stakeout

As told by Alison Santos

3:15: Alison Santos, junior-high detective, here. My friend Zoe asked for my help while Max is out of town visiting his aunt, and that's why I'm hidden underneath the metal bleachers at the side of Whispering Meadows' indoor community pool. The facts on the case: someone in Zoe's swimming class has dumped bright purple food coloring in the pool in each of the last two sessions. The water had to be drained each time, which is a huge waste, and pool officials are threatening to cancel the class if the color dumping doesn't stop.

I'm here to look through the spaces of the bleacher benches, jot down everything that goes on in my trusty notepad, and see if I can catch the culprit red-, or in this case, purple-handed. From my hiding spot I get a great view of everything, from the door of the change rooms at the shallow end of the pool to the diving board at the deep end. I can also see through the wall of windows on the opposite side of the pool.

Class starts in fifteen minutes. I had to get in here before anyone else so I wouldn't be seen. The bad news is it's dirty and steamy under these bleachers. The good news is I've got some awesome stakeout food.

3:18: This just in: cheese puffs are GOOD!

3:20: We have activity at poolside. Alex Rodriguez, our school's resident overachiever, just came out of the change room holding a cell phone.

3:23: Here's what he had to say as he walked around the pool, stopping only once on the other side of the diving board to tie his shoe:

Mom? Hi, it's Alex. Yes, I'm at swimming class. That's what I need to talk to you about. I need to change classes. Why? Because I can't be in the same swimming class as my little sister! Katlyn is always hanging around me in the pool and always wants to be my partner for stuff. It's embarrassing!
Uh...hello? Okay. Yes, Mom. Sure. Bye.

3:24: Alex was steaming mad as he hung up the phone. Looks like we have suspect #1. Maybe getting this class canceled is his backup plan if he can't convince his mom to put him in a different one.

3:25: Busy place! Carylin Dell, the class's swimming instructor, just walked from the lifeguard office to the pool deck. She's wearing puffy red nylon shorts over a red one-piece bathing suit and holding a small plastic container and a bottle of purple liquid.

3:26: Ms. Dell just scooped up some water from the pool with the container and squeezed a couple drops of purple liquid into it. She watched the water in the container for a second, smiled, and then walked back to her office. Interesting!

3:27: When Zoe asked me to help her out, she mentioned that Ms. Dell was recently accepted into a national-level swimming club. Rumor has it that she wants more time for training and wishes she didn't have to teach this class. Double interesting!

3:29: Ugh. Too many jujubes...

3:30: Finally! Class is about to start, and it looks like everyone's present. On top of Zoe, Alex, and his little sister, Katlyn, there are the following seven kids: Layne Jennings, Ursula Curtis, Kyle Kressman, Lorrisa Swart, Kate Yoon, Felix Reeves, and Jeff Coleman. All the boys are wearing baggy swim shorts, Layne and Lorrisa are wearing one-piece bathing suits, and Ursula and Kate are wearing suits with board shorts. That means six kids—plus Ms. Dell—could be hiding a bottle of food coloring on them.

3:32: Scratch that! Ms. Dell just asked the entire class to turn out their pockets before jumping in the pool. Kyle and Alex refused at first (Alex mumbled in his deep voice that it was a "violation of personal rights and freedoms"), but everyone did it eventually. Verdict: no food coloring.

3:33: Everybody in the pool!

3:35: Zoe just waved at me. (Note to self: teach her the meaning of the word "incognito.") Luckily, I don't think anyone noticed.

3:41: Early excitement: Kyle just got caught splashing water in Lorrisa's eyes, and Ms. Dell kicked him out of the class. From what Zoe tells me, this happens a lot—Kyle's our school's biggest prankster. Looks like he goes on the suspect list, too. If he sticks around...

3:42: Kyle walked over me on the bleachers to get his towel and dripped pool water all over me. So...GROSS.

3:47: Class has resumed. They're learning the backstroke. Ms. Dell is telling everyone to make sure that their heads are back, their backs are arched, and their toes are down in the water. This is the best swimming class I've ever taken!

3:50: Uh-oh. Junior-high super-bully Basher McGintley just walked by the windows outside. Please tell me he's not coming in here...

3:55: Oh MAN! Not only is Basher in the pool area, but he chose a seat on the bleachers RIGHT ABOVE ME.

3:56: Zoe told me to look out for this: Basher often shows up for the 4:30 free swim, and lately he's been showing up early.

3:58: Enough bashing Basher. On with the stakeout! Ms. Dell asked everyone to partner up, and something very intriguing happened. Here's how it went down:

> **Ms. Dell:** Okay, class, split off into partners. We're going to swim a quick backstroke relay race.
>
> **Katlyn:** Alex! Let's be partners! We'll be the best team here!
>
> **Felix** (mocking Alex): Oooooh, Alex! You're the best!
>
> **Jeff:** Yeah, Alex. You're the best big brother ever!
>
> **Alex:** Shut up, you guys. I hate this class!

3:59: Alex's outburst sent Katlyn racing for the change room with tears streaming down her face.

4:01: KATLYN JUST RAN OUT OF THE CHANGE ROOM AND THREW SOMETHING INTO THE POOL! CASE CLOSED? HAVE I BEEN SITTING UNDER A SET OF BLEACHERS FOR FORTY-FIVE MINUTES FOR NOTHING?!!!

4:02: False alarm. It was just Alex's cell phone, which, of course, will never work again.

4:04: Undaunted, Ms. Dell has gotten Katlyn back in the pool and is still trying to organize the relay race. She paired Alex with Jeff and Felix with Katlyn and told everyone to go hold on to the side of the pool at the deep end.

4:05: Basher's buddies, Dwayne and Shayne, just showed up. They may be big, mean, and nasty (I could go on...), but at least they got Basher talking when they asked him about the food-coloring pranks. Here's what he had to say:

> I got a real good feeling something's going to go down here today, and I'm glad you guys are here to see it. I'm going to document the whole thing.

4:06: Basher just grabbed something from his bag, but I couldn't see what it was.

4:07: The race is about to start, but Basher's legs are BLOCKING MY VIEW!!!

Ms. Dell: Ready, set...go!

4:08: PANDEMONIUM!!!!

4:09: As half the class was churning the pool into a frenzy and Jeff was taking an early lead, Kyle ran up to the windows on the opposite side of the pool and pressed his face against the glass. A deep voice from the deep end yelled "Look!" and everyone stopped racing and turned to look at Kyle. Ms. Dell hopped out of the pool, pointed at him, and shouted at him to go away.

SPLASH! Through Basher's legs I saw a bottle of food coloring fly toward the shallow end and hit the water.

4:10: And...there it is. A growing purple cloud in the water near the middle of the pool. Was that a click I just heard above me?!

4:11: Basher is standing up on the bleachers now, and I have my clear view of the pool area back. Zoe is looking right at me, and it's clear she didn't see who it was either. Someone above me just said, "Nice shot, Basher!"

4:12: Everyone in the pool is looking around, wondering who, if any of them, is the culprit. But Ms. Dell doesn't look like she wants to hang around to find out. She just threw up her arms and said, "All right. Everybody out of the pool. For good!"

For good? I don't think so.
I'm ready to throw in this food-coloring criminal's towel. I may not have seen who threw the bottle, but that doesn't matter. I know who did.

Alison

Turn the page for the solution.

THE CASE OF THE...
SWIMMING POOL STAKEOUT

Who threw the food coloring?

Alex Rodriguez. He *really* didn't want to be in the same class as his sister.

Clues

- When Alison described her view from under the bleachers, she said there was a diving board by the deep end. She also said Alex stopped behind the diving board to tie his shoe while he was talking to his mom. He planted the food-coloring bottle there while Alison couldn't see him.

- Alison said she saw the bottle of food coloring fly toward the shallow end. That means it must've been thrown from the deep end of the pool, where Alex was. It also means Basher and his buddies couldn't have thrown it.

- Alison said Alex and Jeff were partners in the relay race. Since Jeff was taking an early lead, Alex would've been waiting his turn at the deep end.

- A deep voice called from the water to direct everyone's attention to Kyle's antics. It was Alex using Kyle as a distraction. Earlier, Alison said Alex mumbled in a deep voice about his rights and freedoms.

- Ms. Dell may have been directing attention toward Kyle while he wa making faces at the windows, but didn't throw the food-coloring bo According to Alison's notes, Ms. I was busy hopping out of the pool while the bottle was being thrown

- The plastic container and bottle o purple liquid Ms. Dell was holding before class started were used to t the water quality of the pool.

- Zoe said Basher had been showing early to the free swim. That's how h knew someone had been dumping coloring in the water. The click Alis heard was Basher taking a photo to "document" the food-coloring clou and ensuing mayhem.

Conclusion

Alison emerged from under the bleac to deliver her evidence, and Alex confessed. Ms. Dell kicked him out of the class and, with no more pranks or the horizon, agreed to teach until the end of the year. Basher joined up so h could bridge the time between the en school and the free swim, and Alison. stayed away from junk food for a whil

THE CASE OF THE...
SUSPICIOUS SET

Max Finder, junior-high detective, here. Alison is interviewing movie star Ridge Thorton on the set of his new sci-fi movie, *Ice Planet Okapi*, and she invited me along for the ride.

I'M VERY EXCITED ABOUT THIS FILM, ALISON. IT'S MY FIRST TIME DIRECTING, AND I REALLY WANT TO SHOW PEOPLE I CAN DO MORE THAN JUST ACT!

EXCELLENT, RIDGE. I THINK WE GOT IT. THANKS SO MUCH FOR GIVING US THIS EXCLUSIVE.

CLICK

THANKS FOR THESE AUTOGRAPHED PICS, TOO, RIDGE.

IT'S THE LEAST I COULD DO FOR THE DETECTIVES WHO SAVED MY LAST MOVIE! THAT'S PART OF WHY I DECIDED TO FILM MY MOVIE HERE IN WHISPERING MEADOWS.

OKAY, DUDES. INTERVIEW'S OVER. WE'VE GOT A LOT TO DO BEFORE WE START FILMING THIS AFTERNOON.

THIS IS GORMAN, MY INTERN. I'M AFRAID HE'S RIGHT, GUYS. STOP BY AGAIN SOMETIME.

I CAN'T BELIEVE RIDGE HIRED GORMAN GATES TO BE HIS INTERN! HE GOES TO WHISPERING MEADOWS HIGH, AND EVERYONE SAYS HE'S A TOTAL SLACKER.

WELL, NOT EVERYONE CAN BE AS COOL AS YOU AND ME, AL...

SECURITY! STOP THOSE KIDS! MY SHOOTING SCRIPT'S MISSING!

SERIOUS FILMS CLOSED SET

40

security found nothing in
...ags, Ridge apologized. When
...oticed the script was missing,
...an said he saw us pick up some
...s before we left the trailer.

NEVER
...HOULD'VE
...IEVED HIM.

IT'S OKAY.
EVERYONE
MAKES
MISTAKES.

Ridge told us he'd been making notes
on his script for weeks. When he left
the trailer at midnight, he dropped it
on the table for Gorman to copy in
the morning. They didn't notice it was
missing until after we left the trailer.

THAT SCRIPT HAS THE
NEW SCENES I WROTE...
EVERYTHING! IF IT'S GONE,
WE'LL HAVE TO POSTPONE
SHOOTING SO I CAN DO
IT ALL AGAIN!

THORTON! WHAT'S
THIS I HEAR ABOUT A
POSSIBLE DELAY IN
PRODUCTION?

he lead
...acter in the
...own Malone
...es, Ridge is
...of the toughest
... ever to grace
...silver screen.
...even he cowered
...e face of his
...ucer, Shereece
...mperspoon. He
...lied through
...eeth.

OH, HEH HEH...HI,
MS. WHIMPERSPOON!
THERE ARE NO DELAYS,
MA'AM! WE'RE GOOD TO
GO FOR THIS AFTERNOON
AS SCHEDULED.

WELL, I'M GLAD TO
HEAR IT, THORTON.
DELAYS COST ME MONEY.
AND THEY COULD COST
YOU YOUR JOB! I'LL SEE
YOU THIS AFTERNOON TO
START SHOOTING.

...r Shereece left, Ridge said he had to run
...rference with other movie people. We went to
... Gorman and ask him some questions.

...HEN WAS
...E LAST TIME
...U SAW THE
...HOOTING
...SCRIPT?

YESTERDAY. RIDGE LIKES
TO ROLL IT UP AND YELL
THROUGH IT. WHEN I GOT
TO THE TRAILER AT 7 A.M., IT
WASN'T ON THE TABLE, SO I
ASSUMED RIDGE HAD IT. THAT
MEANS ANYONE COULD'VE
TAKEN IT LAST NIGHT,
AS LONG AS THEY GOT
PAST SECURITY.

DO YOU
KNOW WHO
MIGHT'VE
STOLEN IT?

IT COULD BE A SPY
FROM A MOVIE STUDIO
CALLED FURIOUS
FILMS. I'VE HEARD
THEY SEND PEOPLE
TO INFILTRATE MOVIE
SETS JUST TO MESS
THEM UP.

SERIOUS
FILMS
CLOSED
SET

PROPS

41

SPIES? DOES HE EXPECT US TO BELIEVE THAT?

I WAS THINKING THE SAME THING. HE COULD JUST BE TRYING TO THROW US OFF THE SCENT.

After that, we bumped into security guard Marge Hudson. While she wasn't happy about working with a couple of kid detectives, she filled us in on what she knew.

WE KEEP A LOG OF ALL MOVEMENT ON THE LOT AT NIGHT. MOST OF THE PEOPL AROUND RIDGE'S TRAILER WE REGULARS: ACTORS, THEIR FAMILIES, AND GORMAN.

DID ANYBODY SEE ANYTHING UNUSUAL?

One of our security personnel noted that Gorman was walking with an unidentified person. He had some things to say about Ridge, and they weren't friendly.

RIDGE IS A TOTAL SLAVE DRIVER! I'M STARTING TO THINK I NEVER SHOULD'VE TAKEN THIS JOB!

WHEN THE GUARD CAUGHT UP WITH GORMAN, THE MYSTERY PERSON HAD VANISHED INTO THIN AIR. I DON'T KNOW WHO IT WAS, BUT IT'S DEFINITELY SUSPICIOUS.

EVERYBODY JUST STAY AWAY FROM ME! I HATE THIS STUPID SET!

IS THAT THE STAR OF THE MOVIE?

THAT'S THE STAR'S TEENAGE KID: MARSHMALLOW SWEETEN.

THE CASE OF THE...
SUSPICIOUS SET

Who stole Ridge's shooting script?

Marge Hudson. She was a spy for Furious Films and stole the script to derail production.

Clues

- Gorman said Ridge liked to roll up his shooting script to yell at people through it. Marge had a thick document on her clipboard that was rolling in on itself. It was the script.

- When Max saw the poster showing the security crew for the film, he noticed that Marge's picture was nowhere on it.

- Max also noticed that Marge's hat said "FF" on it. That stands for Furious Films, the name of the underhanded movie studio that Gorman mentioned. The other guards' hats read "SF," for Serious Films.

- Because Marge was wearing the security guard outfit, though, she would've had unlimited access to Ridge's trailer after hours. That's how she stole the shooting script. She was still on the lot waiting to slip out during the security shift change at noon.

- Gorman may have been walking around late at night with a mysterious person, but it wasn't a thief—it was Marshmallow Sweeten. Max realized this when he saw the two passing a note outside the craft services tent. They were sneaking around because Marshmallow's parents won't let her hang out with anyone on set, and she didn't want to get in trouble.

Conclusion

When Max presented his evidence, Ridge and Shereece locked down the set. The real security team got to work and found Marge trying to sneak off. She gave the shooting script back to Ridge and was kicked off the set. Shooting went on as scheduled, and *Ice Planet Okapi* turned out to be the "coolest" movie of the year!

THE CASE OF THE...
GARAGE
SABOTAGE

THE CASE OF THE...
GARAGE SABOTAGE

Max Finder here, junior-high detective and hapless homeworker. It was after school and I was knee-deep in grammar worksheets. Luckily Alison, our school newspaper's star reporter, was around to help out.

THINK OF IT LIKE THIS, MAX: IN THE SENTENCE "YOU ARE UNDER ARREST," THE SUBJECT IS "YOU," AND THE PREDICATE IS EVERYTHING THAT COMES AFTER IT.

NOW YOU'RE SPEAKING MY LANGUAGE!

The knock at the door was o... classmate Ursula Curtis. And didn't seem like she had stop by to offer tips on prepositic phrases.

YOU GUYS HAVE GOT TO HELP ME! THERE'S BEEN A BREAK-IN AT MY HOUSE!

As we walked to Ursula's, she told us she went by her dad's office after school to help him with some filing.

BY THE TIME I GOT HOME, ALL I WANTED TO DO WAS GRAB MY GUITAR, FIRE UP MY DAD'S VINTAGE FLINDER AMPLIFIER, AND PRACTICE SOME SONGS FOR THE UPCOMING BATTLE OF THE BANDS.

I'M GUESSING THAT'S NOT HOW IT WENT DOWN. TELL US WHAT HAPPENED NEXT.

When I got into the garage, I turned on the amp, only to find that the speaker had been blown out. That's when I noticed the broken glass all over the floor!

While I was covering our tracks, Alison was uncovering a clue. She found a hockey ball with the letters "KY" written on it.

THAT DOESN'T BELONG TO US! HOW DID IT GET IN HERE?

KNOCK KNOCK

URSULA? LET ME IN! I FORGOT MY KEYS!

Andy is Ursula's older brother. He goes high school in Twindale, taking a long bus ride there and back every day. He didn't seem too upset about the amp when Ursula told him about it.

DAD NEVER LET ME PLAY WITH THE AMP ANYWAY BECAUSE HE SAYS I'M CARELESS WITH MY STUFF. SEEMS FAIR NOW THAT NEITHER OF US GETS TO USE IT!

CLICK

MAYBE SO, BUT WE'RE STILL GOING TO CHASE DOWN SOME LEADS. DO YOU HAVE ANY IDEA WHO THIS BALL MIGHT BELONG TO?

I'D TRY CHECKING OUTSIDE. KATE YOON PLAYS STREET HOCKEY EVERY DAY, AND SHE'S ALWAYS COMPLAINING ABOUT URSULA'S BAND. SHE SAYS THEY WRECK HER CONCENTRATION.

HEY, KATE, I THINK WE FOUND YOUR BALL!

THANKS, ALISON, BUT IF YOU GUYS ARE HERE TO TALK ABOUT URSULA'S BROKEN WINDOW, GRAB A STICK. I'VE ONLY GOT A LITTLE WHILE BEFORE DINNER.

While we played, Kate told us her first shot of the afternoon went up over the net and through Ursula's garage window.

WHERE WERE YOU WHEN WE CAME BY EARLIER? WE DIDN'T SEE YOU PLAYING.

WELL, I NEEDED A NEW BALL, DIDN'T I? MY OTHER ONE WAS UNAVAILABLE.

SOLUTION:

THE CASE OF THE...
GARAGE SABOTAGE

Who blew out Ursula's amp?

Drew Bacca. He wanted to play guitar, so he used Ursula's family's set of emergency keys to get into the garage, but he accidentally blew out the amp in the process.

Clues

- Ursula said her drummer, Drew, wants to play guitar. That explains why he was fiddling with the guitar and amp in the first place. He was just trying it out while Ursula wasn't around.

- Drew said he went to Ursula's to get his drumsticks, but when Max and Alison talked to him at his house they could see a set of drumsticks on the drums in his living room.

- When Ursula unlocked the side door for Andy, Max realized that it had been locked the whole time. Whoever blew out the amp had a key to the door and locked it on their way out, which means Kate couldn't have done it.

- Ursula said that her next-door neighbors, the Bacca family, had a set of keys for her house. That gave Drew access to Ursula's garage.

- Max and Alison noticed Andy sti[ll] had his school uniform on when he came into the garage. He was just getting home—and didn't have his keys—so he couldn't hav[e] blown out the amp.

- Kate may have left Ursula's place in a hurry, but she wasn't fleeing the crime scene—she was going t[o] get a new street hockey ball. Max noticed the packaging for the ba[ll] sitting next to her hockey net.

Conclusion

When Max and Alison presented their evidence to Drew, he apologized to Ursula and donated the entire contents of his piggy bank to get the amp fixed. After that, Ursula and her dad even taught him how to use it properly to avoid future blowouts!

THE CASE OF THE...
COMIC-CON CON

Max Finder, junior-high detective, here. My friend Alison and I were at the Whispering Meadows Comic Arts Festival. It's our town's biggest comic convention, and it's held at the biggest hotel, the Pilton Meadows.

THIS IS GOING TO BE GREAT! THAT IS, IF WE CAN EVER FIND THE PRESENTATION ROOM.

WELL, IF WE'RE GOING TO FIND OUR WAY BACK I THINK WE'RE GOING TO NEED SOME...

HELP!

WMCAF

OH NO, SOMEONE'S TRAPPED INSIDE THAT ROOM!

BAM BAM BAM

THIS R IS KEE THE DO CLOS

THANKS! GOTTA GO!

HEY... WAIT!

We caught up with the guy we had rescued in the main hall. He was Doug Chang, the creator of *Total Tarantula*, one of the most buzzed-about new comics at the festival. It also turned out that we didn't rescue him in time to save his day.

I WAS SUPPOSED TO TALK TO FANS AND ANSWER QUESTIONS ABOUT MY BOOK, BUT MY HOUR'S UP AND THEY'RE TAKING THE SIGN AWAY. AT LEAST I STILL HAVE MY BOOTH.

WE'LL HELP YOU SET UP.

MAIN HALL

AISLE 4

AISLE 1

KUKUBURI

NOW YOU CAN BE THE BLACK PARA

WIGS

'See DOUG HAN at 10:00am

...e two? Because Doug didn't show up ...me, it looked like the organizers had ...away his booth, too.

...OW HOW AM I GOING ...O SELL BOOKS? MY ...G DEBUT'S TURNING INTO A TOTAL DISASTER.

DON'T WORRY, WE CAN HELP CATCH WHOEVER TRAPPED YOU. HOW DID YOU END UP IN THAT ROOM DOWNSTAIRS?

I didn't know where the presentation rooms were, so I went to the info booth. Someone with long black hair and a shirt that said "Staff" on the back told me they'd lead the way, and I followed. I was checking my phone and not really paying attention.

...ked into the room to find nothing but a basket ...acks and water. By the time I realized something ...wrong, the doors had slammed closed behind me. ...s in there for an hour!

SLAM!

I HATE TO SAY IT, DOUG, BUT YOU'VE BEEN CONNED. SOMEONE WANTED YOU OUT OF THE WAY.

DOUG! THERE YOU ARE! WHY DIDN'T YOU ANSWER MY CALLS?

LESLIE! MY BATTERY DIED RIGHT AFTER I CALLED YOU AN HOUR AGO. WHERE'VE YOU BEEN?!

...e is Doug's sister. He called her to ask for ...after he realized he was locked in the ..., but she was just getting to the hotel ...The trip should've taken her 15 minutes, ...t took over an hour.

SORRY, I GOT HELD UP. I CALLED YOUR CELL, BUT IT WENT STRAIGHT TO VOICE MAIL. ARE YOU OKAY?

HE WILL BE ONCE WE TALK TO TRAVIS, THE ORGANIZER. ALISON AND I ARE ON THE CASE.

Travis runs the local comic shop, Manga Mania, and is the organizer of WMCAF. He was busy answering questions at the info booth, so he didn't have much to tell us, except that Doug disappeared very suddenly after checking in. When no one could find him, Travis assumed he got stage fright and left.

BUT WHY DID YOU GIVE AWAY DOUG'S BOOTH?

I DIDN'T WANT IT TO GO EMPTY, SO I GAVE IT TO KRISTOFF KANE, THE FIRST PERSON TO COME ASKING.

Kristoff Kane is the creator of *Daddy Long Legs*, our town's other cool arachnid-inspired comic. He already had booth space at the festival, but he took over Doug's and had no plans to give it back.

SEEMS LIKE A LOT OF SPACE FOR ONE ARTIST, HUH?

WHAT CAN I SAY? MY BOOK'S POPULAR. WANT TO BUY A T-SHIRT? I'M CUSTOMIZING THEM FOR EACH INDIVIDUAL FAN.

WHAT DO YOU KNOW ABOUT DOUG CHANG'S DISAPPEARANCE THIS MORNING?

NOTHING, EXCE[PT] WAS BUMMED HE [MISSED] HIS PRESENTAT[ION.] HEARD HE GOT S[TAGE] FRIGHT. YOU LE[T ME] KNOW I ASKED A[BOUT] HIM, OKAY?

KRISTOFF AND DOUG WOULD BE IN DIRECT COMPETITION WITH EACH OTHER, SO KRISTOFF HAS EVERY REASON TO WANT HIM OUT OF THE WAY.

EXCEPT FOR THE FACT THAT HE LOOKS NOTHING LIKE THE PERSON DOUG DESCRIBED.

AISLE

AISLE

MAX! ALISON! HOW COULD YOU?!

CRYSTAL?! WHAT DO YOU MEAN? WE DIDN'T LOCK DOUG IN THAT ROOM.

NO, NOT THAT. HOW COULD YOU W[ORK] WITH HIM? DON'T YOU [KNOW] HE STOLE HIS COMIC [FROM] TINA TRAN?

...al Diallo is president of our school's manga club. She told us that Doug and Tina created *Total Tarantula* ...her. Tina couldn't afford to help him get it printed, so he refused to give her any credit.

...G'S A THIEF! I SHOULD BE ...HING HIM, NOT ...ING HIM! EVEN ...E THINKS WHAT ...D IS TERRIBLE. ...HE TOLD ME ...HERSELF!

ONE CRIME AT A TIME, CRYSTAL. WHERE'S TINA'S BOOTH? I'D LIKE TO ASK HER SOME QUESTIONS.

YOU'RE IMPOSSIBLE, MAX!

...DID YOU NOTICE ...TAL WAS WEARING ...TAFF SHIRT? SHE ...D HAVE LED DOUG ...THE EMPTY ROOM TO ...REVENGE FOR TINA. ...R MAYBE THEY'RE ...RKING TOGETHER.

THAT'S WHAT I WAS THINKING. YOU STICK WITH HER. I'LL GO LOOK FOR TINA.

I found Tina's booth, but it took forever to get to the front of the line. It turned out that she didn't have money to help Doug with their comic because she had just paid to print her own 'zine.

TINA, YOU MUST REALLY WANT TO GET BACK AT DOUG FOR TAKING ALL THE CREDIT FOR *TOTAL TARANTULA*.

WHAT DOUG DID WAS UNCOOL. BUT SUCCESS IS THE BEST REVENGE, AND I'VE BEEN SELLING MY OWN STUFF ALL MORNING. I HAVEN'T EVEN TAKEN A BREAK!

Tina's Braina

Meanwhile, Alison was keeping an eye on Crystal. She caught her and Leslie talking anime—not conspiracy.

AND THEN TAILOR SPOON USED HER EXPLODING SASHIMI POWER TO DEFEAT THE GROW-BOTS! IT WAS AWESOME.

I CAN'T BELIEVE I HAD TO MISS THAT EPISODE THIS MORNING! IT STARTED AFTER THE PRESENTATIONS BEGAN, AND I HAD TO BE HERE TO SHOW PEOPLE AROUND.

...and I met back up with Doug to share our info.

...ANKS FOR YOUR HELP, ...S. BUT UNLESS YOU CAN ...VE THAT I WAS TRICKED, ...INK I'LL JUST TAKE MY ...OOKS AND GO HOME.

SHARPEN YOUR PENCILS, DOUG. WE KNOW WHO CONNED YOU.

WMCAF →

Do you know who conned Doug? All the clues are here. Turn the page for the solution.

THE CASE OF THE...
COMIC-CON CON

Who conned Doug?

Kristoff Kane. He locked Doug in the room to steal his table space and keep him from selling *Total Tarantula*.

Clues

- The long metal rod used to trap Doug was actually a leg from one of the tables on the festival floor. Max noticed that one of Kristoff's table legs was missing.

- The thank-you basket on Kristoff's table had Doug's name on it, but Kristoff's basket was missing. That's because Kristoff left his in the meeting room so Doug wouldn't get hungry or thirsty while trapped.

- Kristoff doesn't have long black hair, but his table was close to a stand selling black wigs. Alison even noticed a wig in the garbage.

- Doug said he was conned by someone wearing a shirt that said "Staff" on the back, but the actual staff shirts had the word on the front. That means the con artist was wearing a fake.

- Kristoff had all the materials to make a fake staff shirt and was actually wearing the fake underneath his collared shirt.

- Tina has long black hair, but sh[e] didn't have time to con Doug. S[he] was busy at her table all mornin[g].

- Alison thought it was suspicious that Leslie took so long to get to the festival to help Doug. But w[hen] she overheard Crystal and Lesli[e] talking, she realized that Leslie [was] delayed because she was watchin[g] an anime TV show.

Conclusion

When Max and Alison presented their evidence, Kristoff confessed [to] trapping Doug in the room. He sa[id] he only planned to leave him in th[ere] for the morning and apologized f[or] the crime. Travis gave Doug both [of] Kristoff's tables, and Doug ended [up] selling tons of comics. He then us[ed] some of the cash to buy a copy of Tina's 'zine.

THE CASE OF THE...
TOILET PAPER PRANK

Max Finder, junior-high detective, here. A huge video game store was opening up in Whispering Meadows... right next to the Game Barn, our town's long-time gamer haven. Of course, Game Barn staffers John Chu and Deb Yay had mixed feelings about it: anger and outrage.

WHAT DO WE WANT?

NO EMPORIUM!

AND WHEN DO WE WANT IT?

NOW!

THIS PROTEST HAS BEEN GOING ON FOR A WEEK! JOHN AND DEB MUST BE REALLY WORRIED THE 1-UP EMPORIUM WILL PUT THEM OUT OF BUSINESS.

THEY'RE NOT THE ONLY ONES WHO LOOK UPSET. THERE'S ANA.

Ana Guzman was new in town. Her family was opening the game store. Until now, she'd been making friends and things had been going smoothly for her.

I HEARD JESSICA PEEVES AND SASHA PRICE WERE JEALOUS OF ME, BUT THAT'S IT. NOW IT SEEMS LIKE EVERYONE WANTS MY FAMILY TO LEAVE TOWN!

DON'T WORRY, ANA. TH[O]SE TWO GET JEALOUS WHEN [THEY] HEAR PEOPLE TALKING A[BOUT] THE WEATHER. I'M SU[RE] THIS WILL ALL BLOW OVER SOON.

Blow over? More like blow up. That Friday night, someone covered the Guzmans' new house in toilet paper. Alison and I showed up early the next morning to find a lot of paper...and a lot of press.

IS IT ME, OR ARE THERE WAY TOO MANY REPORTERS HERE?

THE GUZMANS ARE BIG NEWS ON THE SOCIETY PAGES THESE DAYS. CHECK OUT TODAY'S PAPER.

SOCIETY

WHISPERING MEADOWS' WEALTHIE[ST] TAKE IN THE 7:00 PM SCREENING [OF] MY FAIR CADDY.

(FROM LEFT TO RIGHT) MR. PEEVES, MRS. PEEV[ES,] ANA GUZMAN, MRS. GUZMAN, AND MR. GUZ[MAN]

...s out the reporters were pretty useful, too. When one ...ed interviewing an eyewitness, Alison and I listened in.

I PASS THIS HOUSE TWICE WHEN I'M WALKING MY DOG. I WALKED BY AT 7:45 LAST NIGHT, AND EVERYTHING WAS NORMAL. FIFTEEN MINUTES LATER IT WAS LIKE A BATHROOM HAD EXPLODED ON IT!

THAT MEANS THE CRIME TOOK PLACE JUST BEFORE 8:00. THAT SHOULD HELP US ELIMINATE SOME POTENTIAL SUSPECTS.

MAX! I'M SO GLAD TO SEE YOU!

...told us she saw John Chu in ...eighborhood with a gym ...around 6:00, but she didn't ...what he was doing there.

EVERYONE SAYS YOU GUYS ARE THE BEST DETECTIVES IN TOWN. WILL YOU TAKE THE CASE AND HELP ME FIGURE THIS OUT?

...PROBLEM, ...NA. WE'RE ...ADY ON THE ...B. IN FACT, ...FORENSICS ...ET SHOULD ...HERE ANY...

HEY, GUYS!

Zoe may be young, but examining crime scenes is in her blood. A few minutes later, she already had some info to share with us.

I WASN'T ABLE TO PULL ANY CLUES OFF THE TOILET PAPER ITSELF. I'VE TAKEN A SAMPLE AND I'LL GET A CLOSER LOOK BACK AT MY LAB. THAT SAID, I DID NOTICE SOMETHING STRANGE.

MOST OF THE TP WAS THROWN AT THE HOUSE FROM THE GROUND, BUT SOMEONE MANAGED TO WRAP AN ENTIRE ROLL AROUND THE FLAGPOLE NEXT TO THE WINDOW ABOVE US.

THAT MEANS THE PERSON WHO TP'ED THE HOUSE WAS EITHER AN EXPERT CLIMBER OR...

OR WHAT, MAX?

...THE CULPRIT ...ET PAPERED ...OF THE HOUSE ...THAT WINDOW. ...OSSIBLE THIS ...S AN INSIDE ...JOB.

Unfortunately, we weren't the only eavesdroppers out in front of Ana's house that morning.

DID YOU HEAR WHAT THAT KID SAID? SOMEONE FROM INSIDE THE HOUSE DID IT. THEY COULD BE TRYING TO FRAME THE GAME BARN AND GET SYMPATHY FROM THE TOWN. WHAT A SCOOP!

I CAN'T BELIEVE YOU, MAX! YOU WERE SUPPOSED TO BE HELPING MY FAMILY, NOT ACCUSING US. I WANT YOU OFF THE CASE. AND OFF MY PROPERTY!

climbed
and took off
we could get
ing more out
n. But he left
hing behind
ave us a clue.

WEIRD. THAT GUY FORGOT HIS STUFF!

with that, we were out of suspects. ried to catch up with Ana at school on y, but Jessica Peeves held us off.

LEAVE HER ALONE, GUYS. I MEAN, SO WHAT IF THAT FLAGPOLE WITH THE TOILET PAPER WRAPPED AROUND IT IS RIGHT NEXT TO ANA'S WINDOW?

FUNNY TO SEE YOU TWO BEING SO FRIENDLY, JESSICA. RUMOR HAS IT THAT YOU'RE JEALOUS OF ANA'S NEWFOUND POPULARITY.

THAT'S SO NOT TRUE! IN FACT, MY FAMILY INVITED ANA'S OUT TO THE MOVIES THE NIGHT HER PLACE GOT TOILET PAPERED TO WELCOME THEM TO TOWN. IT WAS IN THE PAPER!

MAX! ALISON! YOU GUYS HAVE TO COME WITH ME!

ook us to an empty science lab to fill us in on oilet paper findings.

THIS IS NO ORDINARY TP, GUYS. UPON CLOSER INSPECTION, I NOTICED IT'S SILKINO BLUE!

SILKINO...?

IT'S THE WORLD'S GREENEST ILET PAPER, MAX! NOT TO MENTION THE MOST EXPENSIVE!

THAT COULD MEAN THE PRANKSTER BELONGS TO ONE OF THE RICHEST FAMILIES IN TOWN.

EXACTLY, ALISON. I KNOW WHO TOILET PAPERED THE GUZMAN PLACE.

Do you know who toilet papered the Guzmans' house? All the clues are here. Turn the page for the solution.

SOLUTION:

THE CASE OF THE...
TOILET PAPER PRANK

Who toilet papered the Guzmans' house?

Jessica Peeves. She was jealous of Ana and her status as the new girl in town.

Clues

- Jessica said her family took Ana's to the movies the night of the toilet papering, but the picture in the paper shows only Ana, her parents, and Jessica's parents.

- Because Ana and her family were at the movies, that meant none of them could have pulled the prank.

- Max and Alison saw John at the climbing gym, proving that he'd know how to scale a wall, but they also caught a glimpse of Jessica. She's a climber as well.

- Alison said the culprit belonged to one of the richest families in town. And as the newspaper said, Jessica's family is definitely one of the wealthiest.

- John may have been holding a bag near Ana's house, but that was at 6:00. As Alison said, the crime took place around 8:00.

- The bag John left at the climbing gym had the 1-Up Emporium logo

on it. That's because he's their newest employee. Max pieced th[...] together after they saw John's name crossed off the staff sched[...] at the Game Barn. John was in the Guzmans' neighborhood on[...] the night of the toilet papering[...] accept the job. That's when he g[...] the black gym bag.

- Deb wasn't lying when she said s[...] was suddenly short staffed. The[...] schedule said she worked until 9:00, which means she couldn't[...] have committed the crime.

Conclusion

When Max and Alison confronted[...] her with the Silkino Blue toilet paper, Jessica confessed to the crime. She apologized to Ana and[...] her parents, and even showed up t[...] support them at the opening of th[...] new store—when it eventually open[...] across town from the Game Barn.

The Case of the
Odd Job Shadow

As told by Max Finder

You know how Spider-Man has his spidey sense? Well, I have my mystery radar. It's the feeling I get when a mystery is about to present itself to me, and it's almost never wrong. It was an ordinary Tuesday morning, but my radar had been going off from the moment I woke up. It sat with me while I ate my breakfast cereal, chased me on my skateboard all the way to school, and was still there as I was grabbing books from my locker and getting ready to head to class.

So when I heard a small, squeaky voice calling my name from some unknown place in the halls, I wasn't so much surprised as confused. I recognized the voice, but it couldn't be...could it?

"Myron?" I asked, looking around. Out of a sea of passing classmates popped my eight-year-old next-door neighbor.

"Myron Matthews, reporting for duty, Mr. Finder!" he said joyously.

"I know who you are, Myron," I said. "What I don't know is what you're doing here!"

After some quick questioning, I got to the bottom of the strange visit. It turned out that everyone in Myron's third-grade class had to pick someone to shadow for a day to find out how jobs work in the real world. Myron chose me because he wants to be a detective, too.

"And your teacher let you do that?" I asked. "Job shadow me?"

"Well, I might have forgotten to tell her you're still in junior high school..." he said.

"Myron!" I shouted in exasperation. "Come on. We're heading to the office."

After talking with my school's principal and calling Myron's parents and teacher, I had a plan in place.

"Okay, here's the deal, Myron," I said. "At lunch I'm walking you across the park back to your school. In the meantime, you have to come to class with me. With any luck, it'll be a quiet morning."

"Something will happen, Mr. Finder! I just know it will," Myron said.

"You and me both," I muttered, my mystery radar still blaring.

Five, four, three, two, one...12:00 at last! The bell rang for lunch as I grabbed my math books from the desk, stuffed them into my bag, and pulled Myron out of the classroom as quickly as I could.

"Bye, Mr. Finder!" my classmates yelled after us, mimicking Myron's squeaky voice. Even Mr. Reed, my straight-faced math teacher, had to laugh at that one.

"Mr. Finder?" Myron said as I dragged him down the hall of the math and science wing, pretending not to hear him. "Mr. Finder, I have to go to the bathroom."

"Okay," I said, letting go of his T-shirt. I pointed him toward the bathroom just down the hall from where we were.

"When you're finished, I want you to meet me at my locker so we can..."

"Solve the mystery!" he said. "Got it!" And he ran off toward the bathroom.

"That's not what I meant!" I shouted, but he was already too far off. I headed back to my locker, unwrapped the tuna sandwich I'd packed for lunch, and ate it as quickly as humanly possible.

"Whoa, Max! What's the hurry?" my best friend, Alison Santos, said as she approached my locker.

I explained the whole morning: how Myron had lied to his teacher to be able to shadow me for a day, how everyone in all my morning classes thought that was hilarious, and how I wanted to get him back to his own school as soon as possible. A few minutes later I was finished with the story and my sandwich, but Alison wasn't sharing in my sense of outrage.

"Well, Max," she said, giggling, "it *is* kind of funny."

"Not you too!" I said.

"By the way, where is Myron?" she said.

Just then a strained, frantic voice called out "Max!" but it wasn't the voice I'd been expecting. It was Leslie Chang, our school's resident gossip,

ashion queen, and talent show champ. Word had it that she'd been staying
p late all month preparing a new dance routine for this year's show, and it
as supposed to be awesome.

But right then she wasn't in the mood for bragging.

"Max!" she said as she ran up to us. "Someone stole my homework!"

As if we needed more excitement, Myron chose that moment to show up
gain.

"Mr. Finder! The soap dispenser exploded all over me," he said,
tretching out his navy blue T-shirt to show us the sudsy mess. Our school
ad replaced the dispensers in both the boys' and girls' washrooms earlier
hat week, and they'd all been malfunctioning ever since. Anyone who
anted to wash their hands was getting sprayed with pink liquid soap—no
xceptions.

"Oh, hello!" Myron said, noticing Leslie. "Do you have a case for Max
inder and Associates?"

"Myron!" I shouted.

"Oh, right!" he said, waving at Alison. "Finder, *Santos*, and Associates!"

"I think I'm going to like having Myron around!" Alison said, laughing.

"First of all, Myron isn't going to *be* around—he's going back to school
ight now. Second of all, I'm sorry, Leslie. Your homework problem is going
o have to wait."

"It *can't* wait, Max!" Leslie wailed. "It's due this afternoon and I have no
dea where it is. If I don't find it, I could get an F! If I get an F, I can't
nter the talent show!"

Against my better judgment I agreed to drop by Leslie's locker on the
vay out of the school. It's in the middle of a long hallway. On one end is
he area just outside the school's main office. On the other is the school's
and room. It gets pretty quiet at lunch, making it the perfect hangout
or our school's biggest bullies, Basher McGintley and his goons.

On the way over, Leslie told us she'd spent all night writing out a book
eport on *The Sisterhood of the Traveling Plants* by hand. She'd designed
cover on the computer, printed it out, and stapled the report together
t home, stashing it in her book bag. She dropped by her locker at the
tart of lunch to drop off her book bag and then ran to the bathroom.
Vhen she returned, she realized she'd left her locker unlocked, and the
eport was gone.

"Who would want to steal someone's book report?" I mumbled to myself.

"Yes...who?" said Myron, who was standing right next to me. I looked
ver and noticed he was mimicking everything from my furrowed brow to

the way I was crossing my arms and holding my hand under my chin.

"Stop it, Myron!"

"Yes, sir, Mr. Finder!" he said, snapping to military attention.

"If you guys are done playing Simon Says, I think I have an idea who might've done it," Leslie chimed in. "If I had to guess, I'd say it was Jessica Peeves."

Leslie told us that Jessica, the daughter of our town's mayor and one of the richest kids in school, was mad at her for also choosing to write about *Traveling Plants*. Apparently, Jessica chose it first.

"I didn't think it was such a big deal, but she always wants to be the only one to do things. Maybe she stole it to get back at me!" Leslie said.

That sure sounded like Jessica, and her locker was directly across the hall from Leslie's, but another thought was distracting me. What had taken Myron so long at the start of lunch? Was it possible he snuck off and stole the book report just so he could see me in action?

Deep in thought, I barely heard Alison talking to me.

"Earth to Max!" she said, and I snapped out of it. "I was just saying we should start by talking to some witnesses. Maybe someone saw something."

"Good idea, Alison," I said. "I think I know just where to start."

"Hey, Finder, who's the munchkin?" Basher shouted to the delight of his buddies as Myron and I drew close.

I was beginning to think it'd been a mistake to bring Myron along when he walked right up to Basher, struck his best tough-guy detective pose, and said, "Basher McGintley, I premuse."

"That's *presume*, Myron," I said, stepping between the two. "But yes, this is Basher, bully to the stars."

Then I turned my focus to the bully in question. Judging by the mess on his orange shirt, I thought he'd also fallen victim to the exploding soap dispenser earlier in the day. But then I figured it out: it was sloppy joe day in the cafeteria. Basher had the sticky orange fingers to prove it.

"Know anything about a stolen book report, Basher? Leslie's went missing from her locker a few minutes ago, and we all know you'd rather steal one than write one."

"Good point, Mr. Finder!" Myron said. "What do you say to that, Basher?"

"Whatever, Max. I don't know anything about Leslie's book report. What would I do with it? I'm not even in her class."

"Have you seen anybody hanging around her locker?"

"It's not like I've been keeping a lookout, but the only kid I've seen

anging around Leslie's locker is Leslie. Now take your talking Neopet and
et lost!" he said, gesturing at Myron as he walked away.

To his credit, Myron completely ignored the insult Basher threw at him
nd focused on the case. Maybe there was a detective in there after all.

"I don't know, Mr. Finder," Myron said. "Basher doesn't make a very
icredible witness."

"That's *credible* witness, Myron. But you're right. We need a lot more
ifo and the clock is ticking...for Leslie and for us," I said. We still had to
et Myron back to his school before lunch was over, or we were both in
eep trouble.

With the sound of Basher's giggling still ringing in our ears, we walked
ack to Leslie's locker and found her in a frantic state. While she and
lison were standing around, Leslie had found the cover page to her essay
ving on the ground.

"This was stapled to the rest of my report!" Leslie said as she handed
he piece of paper to me. "It was right beside Jessica's locker, but Basher
ould've also dropped it on his way to the end of the hall."

I scanned the sheet for dead giveaways—like fingerprints or stains of
ny sort—but found nothing. I held the piece of paper out in front of me,
ight at Myron's eye level.

"Notice anything, Myron?" I asked.

"Looks just like a plain piece of computer paper, Mr. Finder," Myron said.
"No rips or holes or anything."

"Thanks for stating the obvious, kid," Leslie said, picking a piece of lint
ff her crisp white polo shirt. "Maybe let the junior-high detectives handle
his."

"Hang on, Leslie. I think Myron's on to something," I answered.

"I am?" Myron said, surprised.

"Yup. In fact, I think you just helped solve your first case. I know what
iappened to Leslie's homework."

Do you know who stole Leslie's homework?
Turn the page for the solution.

THE CASE OF THE...
ODD JOB SHADOW

Who stole Leslie's book report?

Leslie Chang...kind of. She was busy practicing for the talent show and didn't have time to write her report, so she made up a story to make it look like the report had been stolen.

Clues

- Myron noticed that the cover page Leslie found had no rips or holes in it. That means it was never actually stapled to the rest of the book report. Leslie was lying.

- The report cover was nowhere to be found until Max and Myron went down the hall to talk to Basher. Leslie found it next to Jessica's locker because she planted it there to make Jessica or Basher look guilty.

- Leslie said she was in the bathroom when the book report was stolen, but unlike Myron, she didn't have a soapy mess on her shirt. Max described her shirt as crisp and white—not messy.

- Basher said the only kid he saw near Leslie's locker was Leslie. That means it couldn't have been Jessica.

- Max noticed that Basher had sti[ll] orange fingers from eating slop[py] joes. If he'd stolen the book rep[ort,] the cover page Leslie picked up would've had his orange fingerp[rints] all over it.

- Myron may have been missing a[t] the time of the crime, but he wa[s] actually in the bathroom—he ha[d] soap on his shirt after the soap dispenser exploded on him. He wouldn't have been able to go to [the] bathroom *and* steal the book rep[ort] because there wasn't enough tim[e—] Leslie's locker and the bathroom [are] in different hallways.

Conclusion

When Max presented his evidence (and Myron shouted "Yeah!" every time he finished a sentence), Lesli[e] confessed to making up the story. [She] said she was so into preparing her dance for the talent show that she forgot all about the book report. S[he] got an F on the report and missed [the] show altogether, but she learned a valuable lesson: good dancers alwa[ys] do their homework!

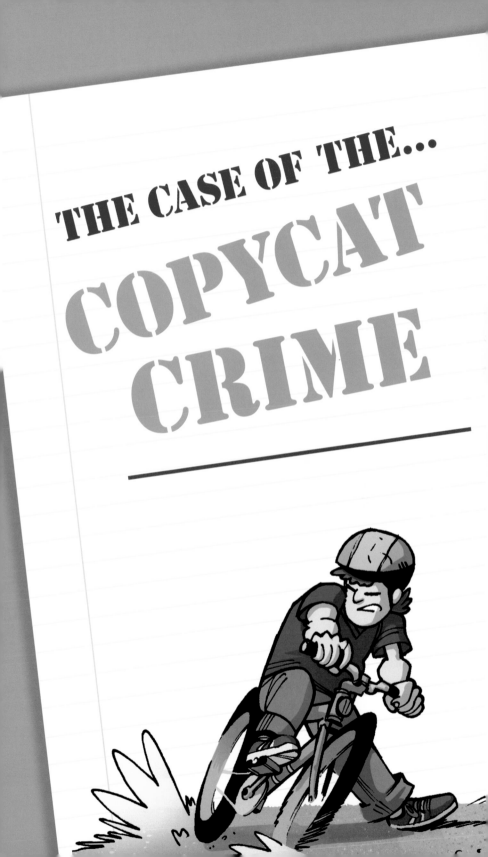

THE CASE OF THE...

COPYCAT CRIME

THE CASE OF THE...
COPYCAT CRIME

Max Finder, junior-high detective, here. Alison and I were hitting the rec center to shoot some hoops on a Saturday morning when we caught sight of a disturbing theme on the bulletin board.

LOOKS LIKE WE'VE GOT ANOTHER ONE, MAX.

BLUE 10-SPEED named blue lightning stolen! HELP!

TEST SCHEDULE

STOLEN YELLOW BMX from SKATE PARK! CALL BEN!

TOLEN!

THEF

STOL from S

REALLY? THAT'S THE FIFTH STOLEN TWO-WHEELER THIS MONTH.

GUYS! SOMEBODY STOLE MY BIKE!

BETTER MAKE THAT SIX, MAX.

BETTER START A NEW CASE FILE, TOO.

Ana Guzman is new in town. She showed up at the skate park to meet friends at around 10:00 a.m. Her bike vanished from the rack during the next half hour, but nobody at the park saw anything suspicious.

THIS IS WHERE IT HAPPENED. I DIDN'T LOCK MY BIKE UP, BUT I WASN'T TOO FAR AWAY. I THOUGHT IT WOULD BE SAFE.

THERE'S NOT MUCH COVER HERE. WHOEVER STOLE YOUR BIKE KNEW WHEN NO ONE WOULD BE LOOKING.

INTERESTING. THIS LOOKS LIKE OIL.

THAT'S TRUE IT FEELS LIKE VU. THIS SE LIKE THE W OF THE BIC BANDIT

The bicycle bandit, a.k.a. Glen Edwards, is an infamous Whispering Meadows thief. He used a leaky car jack to break bike locks and then sold the bikes online. We tracked down Glen's address and tried to pay him a visit. Was he up to his old tricks?

HI, MR. EDWARDS. IS GLEN HOME?

I'M SORR HE'S BEE BACKPACKI IN EUROPE THE LAST T MONTHS. I'LL HIM KNOW STOPPED B

SOLUTION:

THE CASE OF THE...
COPYCAT CRIME

Who stole the bikes?

Mrs. Nelson. She hid the bikes in the woods in order to scare kids away from the park so she could work from home in peace. She used molasses to make Max and Alison think the original bicycle bandit was up to his old tricks again.

Clues

- Mrs. Nelson lives across the street from the skate park, so she knew exactly when the skaters were distracted and bikes were vulnerable. Max even noticed a telescope in her front window pointed at ground level. She used it to watch the skate park.

- Mrs. Nelson said she works from home. That gives her lots of time to steal bikes.

- Layne told Max she was learning to ride, and she was—but not when Nate could see her. Mrs. Nelson said a blond girl was riding late at night. It was Layne. She didn't want Nate complaining about her, so she waited until after he'd left the park to practice.

- When Mrs. Nelson said she saw a boy riding down the street with a skateboard across his handlebars, she was lying. Layne said she saw Nate leaving the park that day o his skateboard.

- Nate may have been using oil to tune up his skateboard, but he didn't use it in connection with stealing any bikes. As Zoe said, the "oil" Max and Alison saw wa actually molasses.

- As the delivery truck parked in driveway suggested, Mrs. Nelso a baker, and that's why she had much molasses on hand.

Conclusion

When Max and Alison presented their evidence, Mrs. Nelson confessed. She explained that she never intended to keep the bikes hidden forever. Because the bikes were all returned unscathed, the courts went easy on Mrs. Nelson. She was sentenced to 50 days of volunteer work...raising money fo new skate park features!

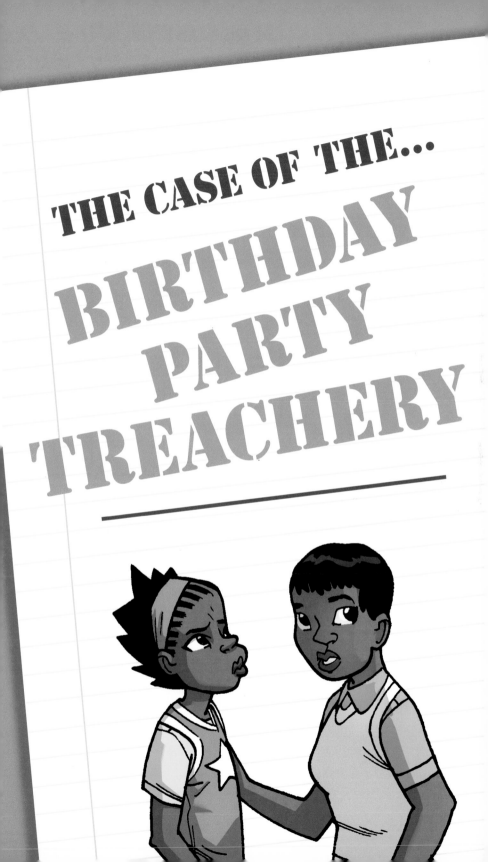

THE CASE OF THE...
BIRTHDAY PART
TREACHERY

Max Finder, junior-high detective, here. It was a Saturday morning on the opening weekend of *Tailor Spoon: Spoonful of Hearts*. Crystal Diallo had rented out our local theater to screen the movie for her birthday, and Alison and I were helping set up.

THIS PLACE IS LOOKING GREAT, YOU GUYS. THANKS FOR YOUR HELP.

OH, IT WAS NO TROUBLE AT ALL.

HEY, CRYSTAL... I GOT A TEXT FROM YOU. LOOK!

IT SAYS FROM ME, I DIDN'T S THAT. SOME TRYING SABOTAG PARTY

HEY ALI! BAD NEWS GOTTA CANCEL MY BIRTHDAY PARTY TODAY, SORRY FOR THE SHORT NOTICE LATER, CRYSTAL :-) FROM 555-583-4348

We tried calling the number, but no one answered, so Alison started looking it up on the 'net. Then things went from bad to worse as Trina, the manager of the theater, arrived for her shift.

CRYSTAL?! WHAT ARE YOU DOING HERE? I GOT A TEXT AN HOUR AGO SAYING YOUR PARTY WAS CANCELED. I ALREADY RENTED THE THEATER OUT TO SOMEONE ON THE WAITING LIST!

WHO?

ME! THANKS FOR DECORATING THE PLACE FOR MY PARTY, KIDS.

Nicole Pilton is one of our to premier princesses. When w asked her to let Crystal hav the theater back, she would give us the time of day.

BUT WHAT IF WE CAN PROVE THAT CRYSTAL WAS SET UP? WOULD YOU LET HER HAVE IT THEN?

FINE. I'M NOT TOT. HEARTLESS. IF Y CATCH YOUR FICTI TEXTER IN THE N TWO HOURS, KRI CAN HAVE THE THE GOOD LUCK WITH

WELL, THERE'S NO TEXT IN HERE. HE COULD BE TELLING THE TRUTH.

EVEN WORSE, HIS NUMBER DOESN'T MATCH THE ONE FROM THE FAKE TEXT. SOMETHING'S NOT RIGHT HERE.

On our way out, we bumped into Dorothy Pafko. She's helped us with lots of cases in the past, and had some info to share when we told her what we'd been up to.

I'M AMAZED TONY WOULD LET GO OF HIS CELL PHONE FOR EVEN A MINUTE! HE'S BEEN GLUED TO IT ALL MORNING AND IGNORING HIS GUESTS.

DID YOU SEE ANYTHING ELSE SUSPICIOUS AROUND HERE?

JUST A LITTLE GRUMBLING. LOTS OF KIDS FELT CAUGHT IN THE MIDDLE OF THE TWO PARTIES TONIGHT, BUT I GUESS THAT'S NOT A PROBLEM NOW.

TOO BAD, THOUGH. I REALLY WANTED TO SEE THAT TAILOR SPOON MOVIE!

TAILOR SPOON? ARE YOU (FRIENDS WITH CRYSTAL? I (CARE WHAT MY BROTHER S SHE BOOKED HER PARTY TO WITH HIM. AND YOU CAN T HER I SAID SO!

WHOA, PHIL, MAN! CHILL OUT!

WHO'S THAT?

TONY'S OVERPROTECTIVE OLDER BROTHER, PHIL. I THINK HE JUST GOT BACK FROM HOCKEY PRACTICE WITH HIS DAD.

THE CASE OF THE...
BIRTHDAY PARTY TREACHERY

Who sent the fake text?

James Tiberius. He is friends with both Crystal and Tony and felt caught in the middle, so he used Phil's cell phone to send the bogus text to get Crystal's party canceled.

Clues

- When James first ran into the theater, he told Crystal he got the "fake text," but nobody had told him that it was fake yet. He was lying. He also told Max later on that he doesn't even have a cell phone.

- James had blueberry stains on his teeth—they were exactly like the kind Dorothy had on her teeth at Tony's brunch. That means James was at the DeMatteo place that morning.

- When Phil got to the brunch after hockey practice, he found his cell phone on a table just inside the front door. It was in the house the whole time he was gone, so James had lots of time to place the text.

- Dorothy said Tony was glued to his phone all morning, but there are two reasons for that. First, it was his birthday present. Second, as Alison noted when he handed

it over, he was using it to look up hockey scores.

- Nicole called Crystal "Krista" at the movie theater. That means she didn't even know Crystal's name, let alone who was on her party guest list or their phone number. She couldn't have placed the text.

Conclusion

When Max and Alison presented their evidence, Crystal called James home and got him to confess. Nicole took back her reservation, and both Crystal and Tony's parties went off without a hitch. The two groups were able to meet up for ice cream later that night, and Crystal and Tony agreed to host joint parties from then on!

THE CASE OF THE...
DAYDREAMING
DETECTIVE

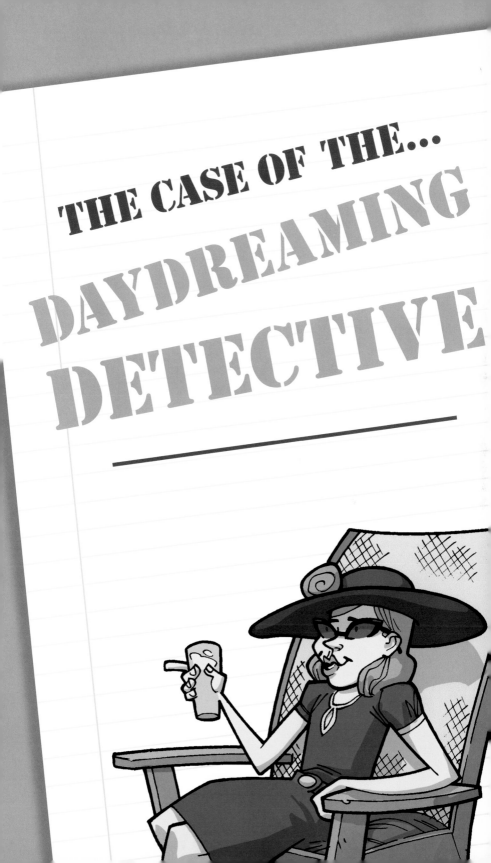

THE CASE OF THE...
DAYDREAMING DETECTIVE

Max Finder, junior-high detective, here. It was a typical summer night in Whispering Meadows: streetlights buzzing, crickets chirping, and me...hard at work trying to catch a jewelry thief.

I'd done all the research, talked to all the suspects, but I couldn't put the clues together to make any sense.

I was determined to solve the case if it took all night, but...

ASLEEP ON THE JOB AGAIN, EH, FINDER?

HARDLY, SANTOS. JUST RESTING MY EYES.

WELL, I HOPE THEY'RE RESTED. I'VE GOT SOMETHING I NEED YOU TO LOOK AT.

WHISPERING MEADOWS
SUN-TIMES
WANTED!
CHANG IN CONNECTION TO THEFT

As soon as I got to the party, Sasha Price started going on about the earrings. She was talking so loudly everyone could hear her.

YOU HAVE TO SEE THEM! THEY'RE WORTH MORE THAN YOUR HOUSE!

I went to the back bedroom to check them out, but the earrings were gone. I heard Sasha coming and I panicked. I took off out the patio doors!

HEY!

INTERESTING TALE. HOW DO WE KNOW YOU'RE TELLING THE TRUTH?

YOU TELL ME. IF I WAS IN THE POSSESSION OF PRICELESS EARRINGS, DO YOU THINK I'D BE HANGING AROUND HERE?

We left Ms. Chang and headed over to the crime scene to talk to Sasha Price, who seemed to be in mourning.

PARDON ME FOR SAYING SO, MS. PRICE, BUT YOU SEEM TO BE TAKING THIS PRETTY HARD.

OF COURSE! FINALLY I GET MY HANDS ON A TRULY ONE-OF-A-KIND ITEM AND THEN IT'S TAKEN AWAY.

SOLUTION:

THE CASE OF THE...
DAYDREAMING
DETECTIVE

Who stole Sasha Price's earrings?

Josh Spodek. He overheard Sasha telling Leslie about the earrings, and he stole them so he could make a profit.

Clues

- Alison noticed Josh signing his number, 23, on an autograph at the ballpark. That matches up with the number on the pin Zoe found on the floor at the crime scene. The pin was actually Josh's earring—he dropped it when he stole Malta's Falconi earrings from Sasha's bedroom.

- Max noticed a glare around Josh's left ear in the party photo of him and Nicholas. It was the flash reflecting off one of the earrings. Max figured this out at the ballpark later when he saw that Josh has his ears pierced.

- Sasha said she had everyone's pockets and the earlobes of every girl checked before anyone could leave, but she didn't say anything about the boys' earlobes. That explains how Josh was able to walk out of the party with the earrings.

- Josh said he didn't see Nicholas a Sasha's party, but in the photo of the two of them Nicholas is clearl reaching out to tap him on the shoulder. Josh was lying to make Nicholas look guilty.

- Alison knew Sasha wouldn't have stolen the earrings for insurance money. She clearly cared more ab attention than money—which she quite enough of as it is!

Conclusion

When Max and Alison showed Josh "23" earring Zoe found on the floo of the crime scene, he confessed. H returned Malta's Falconi earrings to Sasha, who agreed not to press cha and apologized for all the trouble he'd caused. He also resolved to fine another way to make money—after h stops being grounded, of course!

SETTING UP

1. Pick out your favorite Max Finder Mystery— try to find one that has the number of people in it that you want to invite to your party, including yourself.

2. Assign a character to each guest—make yourself Max or Alison, since you'll be the host of the party and they're the main narrators of the comics! Write out a little description of each role (personality, favorite clubs or sports, that kind of thing) on a card so that the guests will be able to get into character right away.

CRYSTAL: character profile

She is a girl who is usually found reading or drawing but is outside a lot because she is a dog walker. She likes to wear bright colors—to match her personality!

The Case of the Birthday Party Treachery

MAX INTRO VOICE-OVER
Max Finder, junior-high detective, here. It was a Saturday morning on the opening weekend of *Tailor Spoon: Spoonful of Hearts*. Crystal Diallo had rented out our local theater to screen the movie for her birthday, and Alison and I were helping set up.

CRYSTAL: This place is looking great, you guys. Thanks for your help!

MAX: Oh, it was no trouble at all.

ALISON: Hey, Crystal...I got a text from you. Look!

TEXT READS: HEY ALL! BAD NEWS. GOTTA CANCEL MY BIRTHDAY PARTY TODAY. SORRY FOR THE SHORT NOTICE! LATER, CRYSTAL! :)

CRYSTAL: It says it's from me, but I didn't send that. Someone's trying to sabotage my party!

MAX VOICE-OVER
We tried calling the number, but no one answered, so Alison started looking it up on the 'net. Then things went from bad to worse as Trina, the manager of the theater, arrived for her shift.

TRINA: Crystal?! What are you doing here? I got a text an hour ago saying your party was canceled. I already rented the theater out to someone on the waiting list!

MAX: Who?

NICOLE: Me! Thanks for decorating the place for my party, kids.

3. Type up or write out a script of the case you want to solve—be sure to make enough copies so that each guest has one to read from. But make sure you don't include the solution to the case!

WHAT YOU'LL NEED

4. Identify any key props you'll need for the case you want to solve. Will you need a skateboard? Some rolls of toilet paper? How about a pretend yearbook with all your guests' faces in it?

This is a great way to reuse old magazines, photos, and cardboard that you have kicking around. Find what you can around the house or borrow from a neighbor, and get crafty for the rest—just check with an adult before using anything someone might miss!

Cell phone Helmet Stuff

Yearbook

What's a crime without physical evidence to look at? Unsolved, that's what! You'll need to create props so your friends can make conclusions on their own and capture the culprit!

5. When your guests arri give them their scrip and props and about fifteen minutes to re over their lines and get a feel for their characters. Give ever a small notepad and to keep track of clues and possible suspects

6. Pick a spot in your house or outside that fits the mood of the crime scene—you can decorate to enhance this! (For example, make a pretend popcorn stand for "The Case of the Birthday Party Treachery" and hand out mini paper bags full of popcorn to help your guests really get into the scene.)

Banner Popcorn stand Posters Balloo

7. Start acting!
Take turns saying your lines according to the script.

DOES EVERYTHING ADD UP?

8. Give your guests the chance to review their notepads. Since you already know the culprit, let each person ask one question (except who the culprit is) to help them figure out who the prime suspect is.

> Real detectives don't just wait for their turn to speak while interviewing witnesses and suspects—they have to listen closely to get the facts. Follow their lead when you're acting! Really listen to the other actors in your scene and then react to them. It'll feel much more natural to you and everybody else.

BALLOT

Suspect: _____

Name: _____

GUESSING WHO

9. After everyone's done asking questions, have each guest write down who they think the culprit is—even if it's their own character! Make sure each guest writes their real name on the paper, too.

DUM-DUM-DUMMMMMM......

THE REVEAL

10. Once everyone's written down their answers, read them out loud. You could have a prize for the winner (or winners!), if you want, or just award them by cheering them on for their mega detective skills!

ALSO TRY...

Preparing two or three cases to make it a full night of whodunit fun.

Or have a friend prepare an additional case so you can get in on the guessing yourself.

MEET THE CREATORS

CREATOR

Name: Liam O'Donnell

Occupation: Creator of the Max Finder Mystery series

Can be found: Writing children's books and graphic novels—visit him online at www.liamodonnell.com

WRITER

Name: Craig Battle

Occupation: Writer of the Max Finder Mystery comics and short stories

Can be found: Editing OWL Magazine—read his blog online at www.owlkids.com/owlblog

ILLUSTRATOR

Name: Ramón Pérez

Occupation: Illustrator of the Max Finder Mystery comics and short stories

Can be found: Drawing for comic books, graphic novels, books, magazines, and whatever else intrigues him

Easy Ways to Use Max Finder in the Classroom

Want to go beyond the mystery on the page? There are all sorts of fun challenges and ways to read the Max Finder mysteries beyond just discovering a story's culprit. Every comic is loaded with lessons on character, mystery writing, graphic novel structure, and more. Here are a few pointers to help set you off in the right direction.

Genre Study:
What makes a mystery? Students can work in groups to research the elements of mysteries—clues, suspects, detectives, red herrings—and present their findings to the rest of the class.

Classroom connections: language arts, media literacy

DIY Mystery:
Using the guide in Volume 3, students can write and illustrate their own mini-mystery, then trade with a partner and try to solve someone else's creation.

Classroom connections: language arts, media literacy, visual arts

Character Study:
Have students study the roles (bully, snitch, prankster) that Max Finder characters play over a number of the comics and graph the results. Is there a pattern?

Classroom connections: math, language arts, media literacy

Comic Format Study:
What makes a comic? Students can work in groups to research the conventions of comics—speech bubbles, caption boxes, paneled illustrations—and present their findings to the rest of the class.

Classroom connections: language arts, media literacy

SOLVE A *MAX FINDER MYSTERY* EVERY MONTH IN *OWL MAGAZINE*